THE NOVELIZATION

Written by Lisa Rojany

From the screenplay written by
Sherri Stoner & Deanna Oliver

PRICE STERN SLOAN
Los Angeles

Designed by Beth Bender
Casper Movie Logo ™
Casper © 1995 Universal City Studios, Inc. and
Amblin Entertainment, Inc.
All rights reserved.
Casper and the Casper characters are trademarks of
and copyrighted by Harvey Comics, Inc.
Published by Price Stern Sloan, Inc.,
A member of The Putnam & Grosset Group, New York, New York.
Printed in the U.S.A. Published simultaneously in Canada.

Library of Congress Cataloging-in-Publication Data
Rojany, Lisa.
    Casper : the junior novelization / written by Lisa Rojany.
        p. cm.
    "Based on the screenplay by Sherri Stoner and Deanna Oliver."
    Summary: When afterlife therapist Dr. James Harvey appears at Whipstaff
Manor in Maine, one of the resident ghosts, Casper, falls in love with his daughter Kat.
    ISBN 0-8431-3854-8
    [1. Ghosts—Fiction. 2. Fathers and daughters—Fiction. 3. Friendship—Fiction.] I.
Stoner, Sherri. II. Oliver, Deanna. III. Title
PZ7.R6424Cas   1995
[Fic]—dc20   94-25837
                                                          CIP
                                                          AC

ISBN 0-8431-3854-8
First Edition
1 3 5 7 9 10 8 6 4 2

The sun fell slowly toward the horizon, turning the sky dark orange and casting strange shadows on the ground. High into the dusk rose Whipstaff Manor. A tall, eerie-looking mansion, Whipstaff stood at the edge of a sharp cliff overlooking the churning sea.

A pair of twin boys skidded their bicycles to a stop in front of the mansion.

"Ready?" asked Nicky, holding up his camera.

"You go first," said Andreas.

"Why should I go first?" responded Nicky, peering through the darkness at the creepy house and then back at his brother .

"You want everyone at school to think we're chicken?" said Andreas. "Come on." Nicky followed Andreas under the fence.

They pushed open the creaky front door. Nicky turned on his flashlight and the beam of light scanned the entryway. The boys were amazed at just how big—and weird—the house was.

"See, there's nothing here," said Andreas.

"Let's just take the picture and get out of here," Nicky answered, feeling goose bumps creep over his entire body.

"Fine, take the picture," said Andreas, posing by an ooky-looking statue.

"Hey, wait—I get to be in the picture, too, or no one'll believe I was here." Nicky pouted.

"No one can tell us apart, anyway. Take the picture!" Feeling creeped out, Andreas suddenly wanted to leave.

"No, you take it."

"No, you."

Out of nowhere came a voice. "Guys, guys, don't fight. I'll take the picture." Before the boys could move, the camera slipped out of Nicky's hand and floated while the voice said, "Say cheese!"

As the flash went off, it suddenly dawned on the boys. "A GHOST!!!!" The flashlight fell to the floor as the boys ran screaming out of the house.

Outside the lawyer's comfortable office, the Manhattan skyline rose into the freezing afternoon sky. A fire burning in the fireplace gave off the only warmth in the room. And the atmosphere in that room was getting chillier by the moment.

"Skip all the charitable donations! What did the old stiff leave me?" demanded Carrigan Crittenden. She was an angry woman dressed all in black—and she wasn't very happy about her father's will.

Rugg, the lawyer, obeyed, skipping through the pages of the will, muttering, "Uh, let's see . . . bobcats, owls, snakes, daughter Carrigan . . . Here you are. You get Whipstaff Manor in Maine."

"And . . .?" said Carrigan.

"And I'm late for lunch," replied Rugg coolly. "If you'll excuse me."

"Are you telling me I spent two days holding his clammy hand waiting for him to kick, and all I get in return is one lousy piece of property?" Carrigan yelled.

"No," said Rugg. "The property was lousy fifty years ago. Now it's condemned." He left the room.

Carrigan was furious. She called after him, "This isn't over. I'll contest the will. I'm going to drag you and everyone else into court!" Carrigan picked up the will and tossed it into the fireplace.

Dibs, Carrigan's own lawyer, who had been listening the entire time, dove toward the fire. How could she burn the deed to her inheritance? Was Carrigan crazy? As Dibs saw the papers begin to burn, the heat brought out some words. The papers included what looked like a treasure map. They must have written this in lemon juice, Dibs thought, as he strained to read the smoking words aloud, "Buccaneers and buried gold, Whipstaff doth a treasure hold . . ."

"Treasure! Dibs, you idiot! Get it out! Get it out!" screamed Carrigan.

Dibs stuck his hand into the fire. He grabbed the map and pulled it out, blowing on it to put out the flames. But it was too late. The map had turned to ashes. Dibs wrapped his burnt hand as Carrigan fumed.

"I knew that place was worth something!" said Carrigan. "There's treasure in that house. . . . And finally, I'm going to get what I deserve!" She dragged Dibs out of the room by his bad hand.

Hours later, Carrigan and Dibs drove up toward the gates of Whipstaff Manor. A storm raged, making the car slip and slide on the steep, muddy hill. With his bandaged hand, Dibs wiped the fog off the windshield inside the car to get a better look. Carrigan made Dibs get out to open the gates. Without waiting for him to get back in, she pressed the accelerator and the car flew through the opened gates. Dibs had to run up after her.

The sound of the car gunning through the open gate reverberated through the old house. Upstairs on the second floor, two ghostly white hands pulled back a curtain. Moments later, the front door creaked open.

"Dibs, light!" Carrigan demanded, clicking her fingers together. Dibs ignited a lighter.

"What a dump," said Carrigan, looking around. Inside, Whipstaff was cluttered with strange-looking furniture.

A carved staircase twisted up into the darkness. There seemed to be too many doors. Where did they all lead to?

"Kind of spooky," Dibs agreed.

"Dibs, you're such a wimp," sneered Carrigan, grabbing onto his arm for dear life. They slowly crept forward into the darkness, exploring various nooks and crannies with the flame of a lighter. After a while, Dibs and Carrigan started to feel almost relaxed.

Then, "Hello," stated a voice out of nowhere.

"Who said that?" whispered Carrigan.

Dibs had no idea.

"Hi, I'm Casper!" The friendly ghost slid down the curving stairwell banister, gaining speed until he flew off and skidded to a stop mid-air in front of Dibs and Carrigan.

Dibs and Carrigan both opened their mouths, ready to scream bloody murder.

"No! Shhh!" Casper warned. "You shouldn't scream or you'll wake the . . ." But Casper's warning was useless. Horrendous, unearthly wails began to shake the mansion.

Casper cringed. "Too late."

Swirling clouds of vapor rose up out of the floor and formed shapes in the air above Casper. The black clouds floated and shrieked. Were they actually forming into . . . ? Carrigan and Dibs were not about to wait around to find out. They screamed so loudly the walls seemed to shake and ran wildly out of the house.

Casper sadly watched the car race away from Whipstaff Manor. Another lonely night with no one to play with.

2

Not far away from Whipstaff, three 11-year-old boys were telling ghost stories up in their room. Casper, floating above the streets, had seen lights flickering through their upstairs window. Feeling lonely and wishing he had someone to play with, Casper flew up to the window to investigate.

One kid held a flashlight up to his face in the pitch dark room. ". . . and they got out and that's when they saw it . . . the bloody hook was stuck in the side of the car!" he finished triumphantly.

"That was really scary," said one of his friends jokingly, rolling his eyes.

"Boring, too," agreed the other friend.

Casper's head popped out of the flashlight. "I know a really scary ghost story!"

The boys screamed and dove into their sleeping bags. Casper, rejected again, floated through their bedroom floor into the living room downstairs.

The boys' father was watching the news. The newscaster said: "Are you depressed? Are you lonely? Do you need some-one to talk to? No problem . . . if you're a ghost!"

Now this is interesting, Casper thought. The little ghost hid behind the father's chair and watched the TV screen.

Now a different man came on. On the screen his name appeared: Dr. James Harvey, Ghost Shrink. "Sure, you can call them ghosts, but the bottom line is they're people, too—or at least they *were* people—and they need help sometimes, just like the rest of us."

Dr. Harvey stopped speaking and the newscaster took over again. "After the sudden, unexpected death of his wife, Amelia, Dr. James Harvey gave up regular psychiatry, as well as, some say, his sanity. Now, along with his daughter, Kat— short for Kathy—Doc Harvey travels from town to town, searching for paranoid poltergeists, scared specters, the depressed and the dead, trying to help them."

As Kat came on screen, Casper perked up behind the chair. He'd never seen anyone so pretty. A reporter was really bugging the dark-haired Kat, trying to get an interview with her.

"What do you feel about what your father does for a living?" asked the reporter, shoving the microphone in Kat's face.

"Could you please not ask me any questions?" pleaded Kat, looking down at the ground. She walked faster.

The reporter wouldn't leave Kat alone. "Do you believe in ghosts? Have you ever seen one? Do you love your dad anyway?"

Kat looked up and said, "He's my father, OK? Look, this is my first day of school, and I've got homework. Excuse me."

Casper felt his heart squeeze. "Kat . . . Kat Harvey," he whispered aloud to himself.

The father watching TV jerked around. Had he really heard a voice behind his chair?

Oops! Casper realized that he had spoken out loud. He zoomed in front of the father and pulled the father's cap over his eyes. Then he flew out of the house through the window. He was going to find Kat Harvey. But first he had some business to attend to.

———

Carrigan was at her hotel talking on the phone when Casper zipped through the cable into her TV set and popped on the TV. Carrigan ignored the TV. So Casper pushed it toward her and turned up the volume. When her TV started acting like it had a life of its own, Carrigan finally paid attention.

It was the same newscast Casper had been watching before. An older woman was being interviewed. "My Harry passed away five years ago," the woman was saying. "But he was so miserable, his spirit wouldn't leave the apartment. So I called Dr. Harvey. He came to my house and in a few weeks, Harry left. Smiling."

Carrigan couldn't believe what she was hearing. "You're kidding me!" she said to herself.

Dr. Harvey came on again. He was a tallish man whose glasses made him look like an absentminded professor. "The living impaired are known for haunting us. But what's haunting them? R is for resolution. Everyone needs resolution to be happy."

The reporter interrupted him, "Isn't it true that in each of these cases, you try to find your dead wife?"

Dr. Harvey suddenly looked uncomfortable. "Yes, I do inquire . . . if a spirit has seen her." He tried to smile. "But no luck so far."

The reporter asked, "Have you actually seen a ghost before?"

"I think we all know ghosts are out there," said Dr. Harvey, not exactly answering the question. "I'm just trying to help people. And I'm confident that I am."

Carrigan listened closely as the newscaster finished up the story. ". . . and so Dr. James Harvey continues his work, dragging his daughter along for the ride. This week they're in Santa Fe. But next week? *Boo* knows?"

Carrigan had tried priests, ghost exterminators, even a wrecking crew to rid Whipstaff Manor of its ghosts—all to no avail. All of a sudden she knew how to solve the haunting problem at Whipstaff. She picked up the phone. "Get me Santa Fe. It's a city." Images of the hidden treasure filled Carrigan's greedy eyes. He doesn't know it yet, thought Carrigan, but the good Dr. Harvey is going to do some ghost busting. And fast.

Dr. Harvey burst through the door of the school auditorium. He didn't notice the boy that Kat was talking to when he ran up to her. He didn't notice the happy look on Kat's face, either. She had just won a part in the school play at her new school. And she was finally starting to make some new friends.

"Kat!" Dr. Harvey cried. "We're moving! There's ghosts in Maine!"

The smile disappeared from Kat's face. Another move. Another new school. Another set of new friends to try to make. When were they ever going to stop moving?

3

Dr. Harvey's battered old station wagon was packed with stuff. It flew down the desert highway with an old psychiatrist's couch strapped to the roof. A spunky song was on the radio, and Dr. Harvey was singing at the top of his lungs, trying to cheer Kat up.

Kat switched off the radio, staring straight ahead, her arms wrapped around her pulled-up knees. Her shoulder-length, dark hair nearly hid her face. She felt more sad than angry.

"Honey, I'm sorry—" he began.

Kat ignored him.

"I don't care what they said, you are not demented," said Dr. Harvey. He had overheard some kids talking before Kat had said good-bye to them. "You're a picture of mental health."

Kat sighed. He just didn't get it. "Dad, they were talking about *you*. Try explaining afterlife therapy to a bunch of junior high kids."

Dr. Harvey was still cheerful. "Look, some people go through life never questioning the norm. But we, you and I, we're doing something extraordinary with our lives."

"Dad, 'we' aren't doing anything," she protested. "You are. I've just been bouncing around all over the place with you. I mean, in two years I've been to nine different schools, eaten in nine different cafeterias—I can't even remember anybody's name! " Kat paused, looking out the car window. "I just want to be in one place long enough to make a friend."

"Honey, you will," he said. "I mean, come on, we're moving to Friendship, Maine. Even I might make one."

Kat snorted in disbelief. "Dad, a single guy your age is more likely to be a bank hostage than make new friends. Face facts."

Dr. Harvey peered at her from the corner of his eye. "You sound like your mother."

Kat turned to him in her seat. "You're not going to find her," she said. When was her dad going to accept the fact that her mother was dead? She was never coming back. "Mom's not a ghost, Dad."

"Yes she is," argued Dr. Harvey, stubbornly staring straight ahead. "She has unfinished business. I just can't find her. But this is our chance! Miss Crittenden said she's had repeated visual sightings."

Kat was at a loss. How could she convince him that ghosts were not real? "There's no such thing as ghosts," she muttered, watching the desert whiz by outside.

"Yes . . . there are. You'll see," said Dr. Harvey. Suddenly, he pulled the car over to the side of the highway. Kat sat up, surprised. "Tell you what," said Dr. Harvey, "I'll make you a deal. You go with me this one last time. If I don't find what I'm looking for, then it's over. No more ghost mining."

Kat couldn't believe her ears. "Do you promise?"

"I promise," he said.

Kat thought about it for only a moment. "Deal!" she said, holding up her pinkie to shake on it.

"Deal." Dr. Harvey put out his own pinkie, and they shook on it. Father and daughter were both smiling.

Finally, Kat thought, sitting back in her seat. I'm finally going to make some real friends. And I'm actually going to have a real house. A home! She couldn't wait!

Many hours later, the Harveys came to a sign and a small seaport town. The sign read: WELCOME TO FRIENDSHIP, MAINE.

12

Dr. Harvey and Kat pulled up to Whipstaff Manor. Kat stared in disbelief at the weird old house. The two driveways leading up to the house were guarded by rickety old gates. The house itself seemed to be leaning at odd angles. The crashing sound of waves warned her that the house was perched at the edge of a cliff. The Harveys slowly got out of the car.

"Wow," said Dr. Harvey, impressed. "It's not so bad, huh?"

"If you're Stephen King," said Kat, not too sure if she was going to like this. The house looked . . . haunted.

Another car was waiting for them. A woman walked over to greet them, extending her hand for a shake. "Dr. Harvey, hello!" she cried shrilly. "I'm Carrigan Crittenden. And this is Dibs."

"I'm Dr. Harvey. And this is my daughter, Kat."

"How nice to meet you!" Carrigan said. As Carrigan knelt down to her, Kat felt her skin crawl.

"You too," said Kat, not really sure if she meant it. Kat hid behind her hair and watched the woman closely. There was something just not right about her. But what was it?

"Dr. Harvey," Carrigan went on, "it's just that we're desperate. You're our last hope. This house is infested with ghosts, and I'm at a complete loss."

"Don't worry," said Dr. Harvey. "With time I'll help these spirits move right on into the next plane."

"You bring up a marvelous point," replied Carrigan. "Just how much time are you talking about? Please tell me you just go in and spray the house."

"As I'm sure you know, a traditional psychological cure can take weeks, even years. . . ." began Dr. Harvey.

"Excuse me?" Carrigan protested. "You didn't just say the word 'years'?"

13

"It's conceivable," replied Dr. Harvey, nodding his head thoughtfully.

"No, no, no! It isn't!" Carrigan insisted. "Days is conceivable. Weeks, maybe. Months, no. Years, forget it!" Carrigan grabbed a flower basket from Dibs and shoved it at Dr. Harvey. Then she got into her car.

"I'll be watching you," Carrigan warned. "Closely." The car peeled out, spraying gravel all over Kat and Dr. Harvey's feet.

Kat and her dad just looked at each other in astonishment. What was wrong with that lady? They watched the car disappear around the bend. Then they turned toward the haunted mansion. Their new home.

———

Upstairs, Casper was bouncing all over his room. He was so excited. "It's her! She's here! She's in my house! I did it!" he said gleefully, popping his head through the floor to peek at Kat. "What if she likes me? What if she doesn't? Of course she won't. She might! Hi, I'm Casper, I'm a ghost? No, that's a disaster. . . ."

Casper ran his hand through his head to get a tough, spiked-hair look. "Yo! I'm Casper. 'S 'up? Gimme four!" He sighed as his spikes drooped back down. "No, you need a pinkie to do that one right."

All of a sudden the lights throughout the house went on. Kat had found the fuse box. Casper just had to see her in the light. He flew through the floor to find them.

Downstairs, Kat and Dr. Harvey had finished dragging in their bags.

"I'm gonna scope out a room," Kat called. "If I'm not back in ten days, send the Donner party."

Casper giggled to himself. He morphed himself into the face of the grandfather clock so he could watch Kat as she

14

passed. She entered a room, hit the lights and there they were: three beds in a row. There were names carved into the headboards: Fatso, Stretch, and Stinkie.

"Fatso, Stretch, and Stinkie?" muttered Kat. "Man, they must have had cruel parents. I wonder where Doc and Dopey sleep?" She turned off the light.

Down the hall, Kat opened another door. The room was the cleanest, happiest room she'd seen so far. She stepped inside and threw down her bag.

"Hey, Dad!" she yelled, smiling. "I found my room!"

Casper watched Kat from outside the room. She's chosen my room, he thought happily. Hearing Dr. Harvey approach, Casper vanished.

Loaded down with heavy boxes, Dr. Harvey entered. "Fatso, Stretch, and Stinkie?" Dr. Harvey said, sounding bewildered.

"I have no idea, Dad," said Kat. "This place is the weirdest one yet."

"Well, I don't know . . . this is a nice room," Dr. Harvey said cautiously, setting the boxes down.

Kat threw open the closet door in her room. She didn't see Casper hovering near the floor, trying to hide. She dumped a box smack on top of him. Casper flattened like a pancake. Kat, totally unaware that she had just smashed a ghost, shut the door.

Dr. Harvey pulled out a photo of Kat's mother, Amelia, and placed it on the nightstand. He stared at the photograph with a sad look on his face. He still missed her so much. Would the sad feelings ever go away? he wondered. He pulled himself away from the image and turned to Kat. "Good night."

" 'Night, Dad," said Kat, unfolding her sleeping bag.

"Kat, thanks for giving me this chance," said Dr. Harvey, hugging her.

When he left the room, Casper morphed himself into a pillow just in time for Kat to lay her head in it. When Kat punched the pillow to fluff it, she punched Casper in the gut, making his eyes bulge out. Still not comfortable, Kat threw the Casper pillow into the headboard—Casper's body went all loopy. Finally, unaware that she'd completely beaten up the poor, friendly ghost, Kat got up, unable to sleep. She began to unpack her clothes. Behind her, Casper prepared to introduce himself.

Kat pulled a sock out of an old boot and tossed it over her shoulder—right into Casper's mouth!

"BLECH!" said Casper aloud, making a grossed-out face. Then, realizing that he had spoken aloud, he froze.

Kat turned slowly around.

"Uh, hi?" said Casper with a tiny wave.

Kat fainted dead away.

4

When Kat fainted, Casper panicked. "A perfect first impression!" he chided himself, staring down at her on the floor. "What a jerk I am!" He dove into the sink, turned on the faucet, and drenched himself. Then he sped into the room and wrung himself out on her. The water would wake her up.

Kat came to. Her eyes slowly focused. When she finally saw Casper clearly, she let out a loud scream. She scared Casper so much he screamed right back! As Dr. Harvey came running to the rescue, Casper flew away.

Dr. Harvey burst into the room. His glasses slipped down his nose as he whipped his head from side to side, looking for the danger. He didn't see anything but a scared 12-year-old girl.

"Dad! I saw a ghost!" Kat yelled, her eyes wide. "A real ghost! A real live ghost! I saw a ghost! I saw a ghost!"

"What are you saying?" Dr. Harvey didn't think he'd heard right.

"I SAW A GHOST!" Kat exploded. "He had a . . . a head. A round head and a . . . little . . . he was white and see-through, and he was floating! Don't think I'm crazy like I thought you were, please, I promise you . . . "

"Kat," said Dr. Harvey slowly, "ghosts can't hurt you. They're simply spirits with unfinished business. OK? OK. Now let's see about this ghost." He opened the bathroom door. "No ghost in here." He checked under the bed. "Nothing under there."

Dr. Harvey opened the closet door—and there was Casper.

"Pleasure to meet you, sir," said Casper politely.

Dr. Harvey shrieked in pure terror. So powerful was his yell that Casper was pushed back into the closet by the gale. The closet door slammed shut.

Kat was terrified, but this time for her dad. Dr. Harvey scooped Kat up over his shoulder and stormed out of the room. He ran down the hall, Kat bobbing up and down on his shoulder.

"Dad, put me down!" she yelled upside-down from behind his back. "This is insane! What are you doing? I can walk, you know!"

Dr. Harvey ignored Kat's protests. He burst into a hall closet and closed them both inside.

Upstairs, Casper was banging his head against the floor in frustration. "Blew it, blew it, blew it, blew it!" he said over and over again. Why could he never manage to introduce himself to humans in a gentle way? He really did try! But no matter what, the humans always ran away, their eyes bulging with fear. It was tough being the only friendly ghost he knew.

———

From inside the closet, Dr. Harvey muttered to himself. "Oh, my! Oh, my! This is big!"

"Dad, are you sure hiding in the closet is the right reaction to have?" Kat asked. The air in the tight space was starting to get used up from their panting.

Dr. Harvey looked down at where he had plopped Kat. All he could see in the semi-darkness was her white skin and a glint in her round, dark eyes. "I want you to stay in here and not come out. No matter what you might hear."

"OK," said Kat. Now she was feeling even more scared. As he started to leave, Kat pulled him back. "Dad. I'm sorry."

"For what?"

"Not believing you," said Kat. "Assuming you were a lost cause, talking behind your back—"

"Honey," Dr. Harvey interrupted, "apologize later." Kat could tell he was still heavily panicked.

"OK," Kat said, watching her dad close the door. She was alone. In a closet. That was not a good thing. Not in this weird place.

Still hating himself for startling Kat and her dad, Casper suddenly froze. A gust of strong wind whooshed through the house. "Oh no!" he said, and zoomed past the fuse box. The whoosh Casper caused made the fuse box fly open and all the fuses shut down. The house went dark. Faster than the speed of light, Casper flew through the front door and blocked the entrance to Whipstaff. And not a moment too soon.

A phantom shape began to materialize in front of the door. Three ghosts suddenly appeared. Laughing like crazy, the three phantoms were loaded down with racing forms, cigars, and betting stubs. One was even wearing the winning horse's wreath around his neck.

The tallest ghost, Stretch, spoke. "Man-o-man, them ponies run faster when we go down to the race track."

The fat ghost laughed. "Hey, horsy . . . BOO!"

All three ghosts burst into laughter. Casper, trying very hard to look calm and casual, joined in.

"Hey guys! Have fun?" asked Casper.

The smelly ghost, Stinkie, moved to within an inch of Casper's face. "On a scale of one to ten—ten being fun and one being you—yeah, we had fun." He laughed as Casper politely waved away the stench, forcing a laugh himself.

"Hey, bulbhead," said Stretch, "why ain't you in there doin' your chores?"

"Where's dinner?" Fatso said. "I'm starvin'. Look at me, I'm wastin' away here."

"Hey, I know," said Casper, "why don't you guys relax out here and tonight we'll eat al fresco?"

"Sounds great, who's that?" asked Fatso.

"Say, short sheet," said Stretch, "you wouldn't be tryin' to keep us out of the house, would ya?"

"No, no," said Casper, "it's just such a lovely night, I thought we'd eat under the harvest moon."

The three ghosts began to sing. Stretch toe-punted Casper, sending him rocketing into the night sky. Casper's outline disappeared against the ball of the perfect white moon. For a second, a puff of dust appeared on the moon.

The main door to Whipstaff opened to admit the Ghostly Trio. They floated in. Stretch suddenly stopped short, arms out, holding the others back. "Hey, Fatso, you smell somethin'?" he asked.

"Yeah," said Fatso, pointing to Stinkie.

"No, besides him."

All three ghosts shut up as a voice wafted toward them. "If anyone can hear me . . . I'm Dr. James Harvey. Thank you for welcoming me. I would like to make contact with you. . . ." Dr. Harvey said, unaware he was being stalked by three of the unfriendliest ghosts in the universe.

5

Dr. Harvey was on a serious ghost hunt. Kat was still upstairs locked in the closet. He had to protect her! Holding a flashlight, Dr. Harvey crept carefully down the hall.

The Ghostly Trio was watching his every move. They sneaked up behind Dr. Harvey, who was stopped in the hall.

Sensing something making his neck hairs quiver, Dr. Harvey did an about face. There were all three ghosts: one tall, one fat, and one so stinky Dr. Harvey choked in just enough air to scream in terror and faint. One by one, the three ghosts dove right into his mouth!

Closed up in the hall closet, Kat heard the scream. What was wrong with her dad? Was the ghost trying to hurt him? Would she get out of this closet alive? She tried to open the door, but it was stuck!

"Dad! Dad!" she yelled, struggling against the door. She couldn't get it to budge.

When Dr. Harvey awoke, all he knew was that his mouth tasted terrible! He walked into the bathroom, where he stood in front of the sink and splashed water onto his face. He looked at his reflection, trying to calm down. It wasn't until he reached for a towel that he noticed. The face looking back at Dr. Harvey, atop Dr. Harvey's own shoulders, was that of a famous actor.

No, it couldn't be, could it? Dr. Harvey strained closer to the mirror to get a better look. The reflection suddenly morphed into a famous comedian's face.

Before Dr. Harvey could blink it away, the face changed again. And again. Then the reflection in the mirror morphed back into Dr. Harvey's own face. Dr. Harvey screamed! This was all too much!

He staggered away from the mirror. His foot landed right into an old sludge-filled bucket. He tried to get his balance by grabbing onto the shower curtain. The curtain came down—and there was Fatso! The shower going full blast, the chubby ghost was wearing a shower cap and lathering up with soap on a rope. Water went straight through him! Fatso screamed and covered himself in a show of fake modesty. Dr. Harvey reeled back toward the door. When he turned around, he saw the door get bigger, then smaller, bigger then smaller. Panicked, Dr. Harvey ran in the other direction. The bucket was still on his foot. And the ghosts were in hot pursuit.

—— ——

Kat couldn't stand being locked up in that closet one second more. With a mighty push, Kat finally shoved open the closet door. Stinkie immediately saw her and raced over. He slammed the closet door shut on her again.

"Hey, boys," Fatso called out, "we got a closet case here."

Inside the closet, Kat could hear the commotion. Who did those voices belong to? Was her dad in big trouble? Was she ever going to get out of this dark prison?

—— ——

Dr. Harvey raced toward the stairway. What he saw stopped him cold: from down the hall, a large lump under the carpet sped directly at him! Dr. Harvey panicked as Stinkie popped out from under the carpet, right in front of him. The ghost was dressed in a delivery person's uniform.

"Smell-o-gram!" yelled Stinkie, letting out a loud, stinky

burp cloud. Stinkie laughed with glee at the horrified look on Dr. Harvey's face.

Dr. Harvey got dizzy from the stench. He tripped over the vacuum cleaner. Grabbing onto the stair carpet to stop himself, Dr. Harvey rolled down the stairs. In the process, he rolled himself up like a burrito. The human burrito bumped and thumped, then unrolled right in front of the three ghosts—who were armed with sabers!

"All for one and one for all!" they chimed in unison.

"Catch your pants before they fall!" said Stretch as he slashed off Dr. Harvey's slacks. Dr. Harvey raced into the bathroom and slammed the door shut. Inside, he looked around for something to defend himself from the three crazed phantoms.

Outside, the Ghostly Trio passed around high-fives.

"You are good!" slapped Stinkie.

"No, it's you," slapped Stretch.

"Are we scary or what?" slapped Fatso.

Out of nowhere, Dr. Harvey suddenly reappeared. He held a toilet plunger up in the air. Stinkie, Fatso, and Stretch smiled. They couldn't wait to pulverize the good doctor.

———

After the Ghostly Trio shot him to the moon, it took Casper a while to get back. As he floated down to earth, he was just in time to see Stretch knock Dr. Harvey's plunger away. From down the hall came a muffled voice, "Dad!" It was Kat!

"Kat!" Casper whispered. Where was she? He flew away in search of her just as Dr. Harvey noticed the vacuum cleaner.

Inside the closet, Kat pulled back for one last, huge push at the closet door. As she went for it, Casper opened the door, sending her flying right into him.

The friendly ghost was squashed flat under her. They were face to face.

"You OK?" asked Casper.

Kat screamed and jumped up. She saw her father holding on to the vacuum cleaner hose as the ghosts got closer and closer to him. At the top of the stairs, Kat eyed the vacuum cord. It was unplugged. Her dad was in big trouble. Kat leaped and grabbed for the plug. She plugged it into the wall socket just as Dr. Harvey flipped the vacuum on. The vacuum revved up and sucked Stretch, Fatso, and Stinkie into the nozzle.

Dr. Harvey, suddenly feeling more tired than he had ever been before, dropped the vacuum hose. At the rate this day was going, these ghosts were going to make him really crazy.

Before Casper could say a word, Dr. Harvey called out Kat's name. She ran toward him.

After they hugged, Dr. Harvey said, "We need to regroup." They needed a plan.

6

Early the next day, the morning sun illuminated Whipstaff Manor's gloomy exterior. Inside, clutching a hand-held vacuum cleaner, Kat walked slowly toward the kitchen. She was scared, but it was her first day at a new school. She had to eat something!

Very slowly she pushed open the door. What she saw shocked her. The table was set with a tablecloth and silverware was neatly laid out. There were bright flowers in a vase.

Suddenly Casper zipped into view, inches from Kat. "Good morning!" he said cheerfully. Kat inhaled, about to scream. Casper zoomed over and wrapped himself around her head like a white muffler. Kat tried to pry him off her mouth.

Casper's eyes peered desperately into hers. "Please-don't-scream!-I-promise-I-won't-hurt-you!" he said quickly. "I'm a ghost, yes, I admit that—but I'm a friendly ghost! You have to trust me! If you scream, you'll wake up my uncles! And they get awfully cranky. Last night, for example? They were very well rested. You can only imagine how bad it can get."

Their eyes were locked into each other's.

"I'm gonna let go now, OK?" said Casper. Kat nodded. Slowly Casper unwrapped himself. He smiled, floating in front of her.

Still in shock, Kat touched her face. "You're so cold," she said.

"I know," Casper replied. "But it's great in summer!" He flew over to Kat's chair and pulled it back for her to sit. Kat kept her eyes both on him and on the hand-held vacuum.

"Gosh, I can see right through you," she said to him.

"It's a symptom of not having any skin."

"What are you . . . made of?" she asked.

"Well," Casper paused, thinking, "you know that tingly feeling you get when your foot falls asleep?" Kat nodded. "I think I'm made of that."

A timer dinged. Kat watched as Casper made her eggs and fresh juice for breakfast. When he floated over with a glass, she stared at his semi-invisible form.

"Go ahead," Casper said, holding out his hand, palm out.

"Can you hurt me?" she asked.

"No."

"Can I hurt you?" she said.

"No."

She raised her palm slowly. Their hands met and passed through each other! Kat smiled, amazed. "Cool!"

Casper suddenly looked at the door. There was Dr. Harvey, timidly edging himself into the room.

"Morning, Dr. Harvey. Like some breakfast?" Casper said.

Dr. Harvey nodded slowly, his face white and his mouth grim. Casper loaded up his plate.

"How about a paper?" Casper asked.

"Sure . . ." said Dr. Harvey, getting more shocked by the second.

"Be right back," sang Casper, as he zoomed out of the room.

Just then, the sound of helicopters filled the room. It grew louder and louder. Dr. Harvey and Kat peered around nervously, seeing nothing.

Nothing until Stretch, Fatso, and Stinkie flew down from the ceiling. The points on their heads were spinning like propellers. They landed across the table from the Harveys.

"I love the smell of fleshies in the morning," Stretch said, smiling menacingly.

The Trio burst into howling laughter. Suddenly, the kitchen window shade snapped up, flooding the room with sunlight.

The sunlight hit the ghosts—and streamed right through their translucent bodies. They began to cringe and curl. Screeching piercingly, the uncles called out, "I'm melting. I'm melting. Auntie Phlegm, Auntie Phlegm! What a world . . ." They fizzled into the floor. Where there once had been three horrendous ghostly blobs, there was now nothing.

"I guess they crossed over," said Dr. Harvey, "They're gone."

"Guess again, bonebag!" Stretch said appearing out of nowhere.

Dr. Harvey shifted protectively toward Kat, then said, "Fellas, good morning!"

Stretch ignored Dr. Harvey and yelled, "CASPER!"

Casper blasted in through an open window, carrying a stack of newspapers for Dr. Harvey. Just as Casper was about to offer one to Dr. Harvey, Stretch sneered, "How dare you serve these air sucking intruders before us?"

"I was just—" protested Casper.

"GIMME MY MEAL!" interrupted Stretch.

Casper flew out of the room. He floated back carrying a tray piled high with junk food. The second Casper set the tray down, the Trio opened their mouths three times normal size. They began shoveling food in with both hands. The food fell straight through their bodies and splattered on the floor. The Harveys were disgusted. Casper floated in with a broom and tried to clean up. The ghosts discussed Casper as if he weren't even there.

"You know what his problem is?" said Stretch. "Casper's got no respect for us."

"And after all we done for the little glow worm," Fatso agreed.

"He's got plenty of respect for the livin', I'll tell ya that," Stinkie said.

"Yeah, and what's so great about bein' alive?" said Stretch.

"Nothin!" agreed all three.

"Stinkie," said Stretch, "had a toothache since you been dead?"

"Not a one."

"Fatso, you wake up with mornin' breath?" asked Stretch.

"I don't wake up with no breath at all," Fatso said. "Hey! Stop cleaning that floor!" Stretch yelled at Casper. "It used to be dirty enough to eat off of!"

Kat listened. She couldn't believe what she was hearing. Enough was enough. "You guys are disgusting, obnoxious creeps," she finally said.

"Thank you!" chimed all three.

"What's your problem?" Kat demanded. "He was just cleaning the floor."

"Shuddup, skinbag," Stretch said to her.

"Kiss off!" Kat said.

"Drop dead!" said Stretch.

"Get a grave!" retorted Kat.

Dr. Harvey interrupted. "Kat, honey, you have school. You don't want to be late your first day." He steered her out the door with a kiss. Turning back, he gave himself a pep talk. "Go ahead," he whispered to himself, "you've been doing ghost therapy for years. Only this time it's for real." He walked back in to confront the uncles. "All right, guys. We obviously started off on the wrong foot here," Dr. Harvey said, hands on his hips. "Now you know and I know that you fellas shouldn't be here. So I'll tell you what. I'll let you finish your meal. Then we can meet in my office and start the process of crossing over. What do you say?"

From every direction of the room globs of food flew right at Dr. Harvey. In seconds, he was dripping with food muck and slime from head to toe. This day was simply not starting out as well as he had hoped.

7

Kat wound her way through the seaside village of Friendship on her way to another first day at another new school. Other kids rode past her on their bicycles. Kat rounded a bend and a girl zipped by, nearly knocking her over.

"Hey, watch it!" snarled the girl.

Kat jumped aside as the girl pedaled away.

"Hey, Amber, wait up!" called a voice behind her. Kat turned to see a cute seventh-grade boy pedaling past her. They made eye contact. Kat surveyed his shaggy hair and sparkly eyes. He gave her a small smile. Kat smiled back at him. Maybe school wasn't going to be so bad after all.

Casper had tried to follow Kat to school. He made her lunch, tried to give her directions for a shortcut, and even wanted to carry her backpack. But Kat convinced him that she didn't need a ghost—even a friendly one—coming to her new school with her.

Once at school, Kat was lost in the sea of students. All shapes and sizes, they whirled past her in a rush of colors and chattering voices. They all said hello to each other, but not to her. She had never felt so alone. As she approached her locker, Kat almost jumped out of her skin. A white ghostly shape was floating toward her. She caught her breath. It was only a gauze ghost for a Halloween display.

Relieved, Kat found her locker and tried the combination. It didn't work. She tried again. No success. A hand reached over her and hit the locker twice; it popped open. Surprised, Kat recognized the guy who had smiled to her from his bike.

"I had this locker last year," he said shyly.

"Thanks," said Kat with a smile.

"Name's Vic."

"Kat." She blushed.

Their smiles were interrupted by a slammed locker. "You coming, Vic?" said Amber, the girl who had nearly knocked Kat over on the way to school. As she looked Kat over from head to toe, Amber did not look one bit pleased.

Five minutes later, Kat was inside Mr. Curtis's class. She sat alone, far in the back of the room. Please let this day go fine, she thought. She stared straight ahead at the front of the room.

"OK, gang, put a lid on it," said Mr. Curtis. The class quieted down. "I have some announcements. First, the repairs to the gym are taking longer than planned, so it looks like we're going to have to push back the Halloween dance a couple of months."

The class groaned their disappointment. Amber raised her hand. "As most of you know, my parents have almost finished the boat house, so I'm sure it would be no problem to have the party at my place."

The students clapped politely.

"Great, that's done," said Mr. Curtis. "Secondly, we have a new student today that I want you all to meet," he checked the computer printout. "Harvey Kathleen."

Kat felt like dying. Could it possibly get worse? Mr. Curtis looked at everyone. Everyone stared back at him. Finally it was clear she had to do something before they all thought she was retarded. Kat shyly raised her hand.

"Oops," said Mr. Curtis, when he saw that Harvey Kathleen was a girl. He checked the printout again. "Let that teach us all the importance of a comma. Say hi to Kathleen Harvey. Why don't you come up front for a moment?"

It just got worse, Kat thought to herself as she slowly stood. The walk to the front of the class seemed to take forever. She tried to look casual. As she passed Amber, Amber snickered into her hand, "Harvey . . ."

Kat finally made it to the front. "So, anything special you want to tell us about yourself, Kathleen?" Mr. Curtis said.

"Well, everybody calls me Kat, and . . ." from the back, Amber meowed nastily. Kat continued, "I guess I just moved here from Santa Fe with my dad and Friendship seemed like a pretty . . . friendly place."

A couple of snores sounded from the class. Underneath the desks, where no one could see, the students' shoelaces were being magically tied together by invisible hands.

"So, where are you guys living?" asked Mr. Curtis.

"Oh, in a house . . ." Kat said, trying to avoid the question. "Just outside of town, kind of up a hill."

"The old Cooper house?" asked Mr. Curtis.

"Well, no," said Kat.

"The Pierce place?"

"No."

"The O'Donnell's?"

Kat shook her head, no.

"Not Whipstaff?" said Mr. Curtis with a small smile.

"Oh, you know it?" Kat said weakly.

"You actually live there?" asked a student, amazed.

"Well, yeah, I mean, I know it looks kind of funky outside and everything. But inside, it's kind of cool," said Kat, trying to smile.

"Yeah, if you drink blood," replied the same student. Everyone burst out into laughter.

Kat looked toward the back of the class, only to see Casper's head appear in a poster of Mount Rushmore. Casper winked at her. Kat turned white.

"Hey, Mr. Curtis," said another student, standing. "Check this out. We're dead for the Halloween dance, right? Well, this girl's got a seriously creepy house with room to spare!"

The class agreed in a loud chorus of "yeahs!"

Amber stood. "Wait a minute. Wait a minute. Everybody just said we were going to have the party at my house," she said, glaring at Kat. The room was silent. "OK, let's take a vote. Everyone who wants it at my house, raise your hand." No one moved. Amber stared Vic down until he slowly began to raise his hand.

"Whipstaff?" said Mr. Curtis.

Everyone raised their hands. "So, what do you say, Harvey?" asked Mr. Curtis. Kat didn't have a choice. Halloween at her house. Great. Just great.

Inside Friendship's city hall, Carrigan and Dibs were poring over the layout of the rooms in Whipstaff Manor. Every hour that the ghosts were still in the house made her want her hidden treasure more.

"Hey, Dibs," said Carrigan, "what are these?"

Dibs took the layout. "Charcoal sketches?" he muttered stupidly. "Beautiful shading there . . ."

"No, no, you idiot, look!" Carrigan pointed to a part of the mansion's layout. "Do you see what I see?"

Dibs looked down. "If we break through the pantry, you could add a laundry room?"

"No. Here," said Carrigan impatiently, jabbing at it again. "Why would anyone need a room this size under a house?"

"Safe, protected, no one can get to it," agreed Dibs as it dawned on him.

"Dibs, I think we found what we're looking for—my treasure!" Carrigan and Dibs left in a hurry. They had a house to tear apart. There was treasure to be found, ghosts or no ghosts.

8

It was time to confront the ghosts again. Dr. Harvey was not a ghost therapist for nothing. But these ghosts were something else. He took a deep breath and whipped open the door to his office, announcing, "Gentlemen, the doctor is in."

Dr. Harvey was surprised to see the Ghostly Trio calmly floating over his sofa. Their hands were politely folded in their laps. Dr. Harvey placed a chart on a stand. The letters on the chart spelled out DEATH.

"This is what you are," said Dr. Harvey, pointing at the D. "D. In denial."

"De Nile . . . dat's in Egypt," said Fatso, proud of himself. Stretch whammed Fatso in the head.

Dr. Harvey ignored them, continuing, "E. You feel empty. A. You were abandoned by life. T. Too bad about me, is what you say. H. Heck, what can I do about it?"

"You can forgetaboutit, that's what you can do about it," said Stretch. Stretch and Stinkie popped out of the room. But Fatso stayed, looking quite willing to abandon himself to the therapy, much to Dr. Harvey's surprise.

"Don't be afraid to take this journey alone," said Dr. Harvey comfortingly to Fatso. "All you need is yourself."

Fatso dropped his head into his hands. "Doc, I don't know what to do," he wailed. "I mean, I'm in crisis."

Aha, thought Dr. Harvey. Now we're getting somewhere. All I need is time; with time and patience, I feel sure I can get these ghosts away from Whipstaff and where they really belonged, wherever that was. Before Dr. Harvey could encourage Fatso to continue with the therapy session, the front door flew open and Kat entered, breathless. She walked into his office with an expectant look on her face. "Dad? Can I have a party?" Time had just run out.

—••—

Seconds later, Kat was climbing up the stairs. Casper floated after her. Just then, the doorbell rang. Casper and Kat looked down the stairs. Now who could that be?

Kat opened the door and was shocked to see . . . Vic! "Vic?" she said, breathless. "What are you doing here? I mean, hi!"

"Hey, Kat."

Casper appeared above the doorway, upside-down, to check Vic out. Kat noticed what Casper was doing and tried to block Vic's view into the house.

"Can I come in?" asked Vic, craning his neck to see behind Kat.

"No!" said Kat. She stepped outside and slammed the door behind her. Vic looked at her, trying to figure out what was up. "I, uh, sorry, but it's so much nicer out here in the flesh air. I mean fresh air," said Kat, giggling.

"Did you ask your dad about the party?"

"Yeah," said Kat, "he hit the ceiling, but I think it's going to be OK."

Suddenly Casper appeared behind Vic, where only Kat could see him. Casper pretended to be swinging from a rope. Then he pretended to mock Vic's cool posture. Kat glared at Casper and paid attention to Vic, who was saying, "Cool. So listen, if you're not hooked up with anybody, you wanna hang with me at the party?"

Kat was stunned. This cute boy wanted to hang with her? Cool! "I'd love to," she said, shooting Casper a look of hate.

Casper faded away.

"Cool!" said Vic. "Well, see ya."

Kat nodded. She was totally excited. This was going to be the best Halloween ever. No matter what. And no one was going to ruin it for her. Not even a bunch of wacky ghosts.

———

Vic heard the door close behind him. He stepped through the front gates of Whipstaff where Amber was waiting for him behind a post.

"Well? Well? Did you ask her?" said Amber, impatient to see if the first part of her plan had been pulled off.

"Yeah," said Vic, not smiling. Vic liked Kat. He thought she was nice. And he didn't really think Amber's plan was such a great idea.

"And she actually bought it? What a joke." Amber thought it was the best idea she'd ever had.

"This is really mean," said Vic glumly. "It's not right."

"No. It's perfect," said Amber wickedly. "Happy Halloween, Kat Harvey!" From the moment Kat had snatched the party away from her, Amber had been looking for a way to get her back. If this idea went as planned, Kat Harvey was going to be sorry she'd ever *heard* of a town called Friendship.

9

Upstairs that night, Kat stood happily in front of the mirror, humming to herself. She put her hair up and checked it out. Yuck. She took it down and fluffed it out. Worse yuck. She opened a little jewelry box to pull out a hair scrunchie, only to find a tiny Casper, whirling around like a musical ballerina.

"See," he said. "I'm a good dancer."

Kat took out the hair scrunchie and slammed down the lid. Casper was getting annoying. She pulled her hair up and went over to the dresser. Opening a drawer, she discovered Casper folded up like a shirt.

"I don't even need a costume!" he said gleefully.

Kat slammed the drawer shut and walked over to the closet. When she opened the closet door, a bunch of Casper-faced balloons bobbed in her face.

"I'm always the life of a party!" Casper grinned.

"Casper, listen," said Kat. Her patience was wearing a little thin. "I know you want to go—"

"Come on," the friendly ghost begged. "We'd have a great time together."

"Casper, I have a date," Kat stated.

"What's this Vic guy got that I don't?" demanded Casper.

"A pulse?" retorted Kat.

"Big fleshie deal," retorted Casper sullenly.

"A tan . . ." Kat added meanly.

"Very bad for your skin," Casper coolly replied.

"How about a reflection?" she taunted.

Casper looked into the mirror and saw what he always

saw: no reflection. "OK, OK. But can he do this?" Casper inflated himself into a big C. Then he stuck his thumb in his mouth.

Kat was not impressed, and Casper could see that. What next? He grabbed Kat's hand, pulling her toward toward the open window. She dug her heels into the floor. "Casper, don't! No . . . no . . . no! Casper!!"

Casper yanked her out the window. Kat dropped down. She was hanging by an ankle—which Casper now held in one hand!

"Bad idea! Very bad idea," yelled Kat, freaking out. "Put me down, Casper! Put . . ." Casper didn't listen. With the moon shining bright in the night sky, Casper flew off, taking Kat with him—still hanging by the ankle.

—◆—

High above the ocean, on a lighthouse dome, Casper sat on a ledge. The sea waters churned below and he was watching the slow movement of the waves. Kat sat next to him. They looked almost like two normal friends.

"Casper, this is beautiful," she said softly.

"I come here every night," said Casper.

"Alone?"

Casper nodded. The lighthouse beam flashed across the water and then dipped away again.

Kat continued, "What were you like when you were alive?"

"I was . . . I was . . ." Casper paused, then sighed heavily. "I don't remember."

"You don't remember anything from your life?" she asked.

"No."

"So you don't remember what school you went to? How old you were? Your favorite song?" Casper was silent. "What about your dad?" Casper thought hard. Nothing. "Not even your mom?"

Casper looked up. "Is that bad?"

"No," Kat said. "Just sad."

— ◆ —

Glowing in the light of the candles by her bed, Kat lay propped up on an elbow. It was late. She had survived the flight back to Whipstaff, and she and Casper were still talking. "I wonder why you don't remember anything."

"I guess 'cuz when you're a ghost, your life doesn't matter much anymore, so you forget," said Casper.

Kat looked upset. "Casper, can I tell you something I haven't really told anybody?"

"Mm-hm." Casper watched his favorite girl closely.

"Sometimes I'm scared I'm starting to forget," said Kat.

"Forget what?" Casper was confused.

"My mom. Just certain things. The sound of her voice when she'd laugh, the way her fingertips felt when she'd run them through my hair. . . ." Kat started to drift asleep. "I do remember I could always smell her on my clothes after she did the wash, and when I'd get sad I'd breathe her in so deep." Kat yawned. "And at night when the sheets were cold, her breath would always warm me when she'd whisper to me, so close . . . Casper?"

"Hmm?" Casper wanted to touch her hair, comfort her, so badly.

"If my mom's a ghost, did she forget about me?"

"No," said Casper, "she could never forget about you." He was quiet for a minute. "Kat?"

"Hmm?"

"If I were alive, would you go to the Halloween dance with me?" Casper asked.

"Sure," agreed Kat.

"Kat?"

"Hmm?" She was more asleep than awake.

"Can I keep you?" whispered Casper.

"Sure," whispered Kat, fading away into dream land.

Casper smiled, letting out a tiny sigh. He watched her face in the moonlight. Before he left the room for the night, he leaned over and kissed her on the cheek.

"Casper," Kat mumbled, "close the window. It's cold."

Casper looked at the window. It was already closed. He stared at the photograph of Amelia, Kat's mom, on Kat's nightstand. He imagined what it was like for Kat to have a mom who ran her hand through her hair, comforting her before bed, or giving a hug good night. He couldn't even remember his own mom. As Casper got ready to leave, he looked down at Kat. Her sleeping face held a sweet smile.

10

Bright and early the next morning, Kat bounded down the steps two at a time. Her dreams the night before had left her with a warm, safe feeling and she was raring to start her day. She slapped open the kitchen door with a loud, "Hey, Dad!"

Dr. Harvey nearly jumped out the kitchen window above the sink where he was pouring himself a cup of coffee. His nerves were more than a little frayed from the ghostly goings on at Whipstaff Manor.

"Found your credit card, Dad," announced Kat.

"Oh. Where was it?" asked Dr. Harvey, wondering when he had lost it.

"In your wallet," she answered with a slight smile. "I was thinking I could use it to get this perfect costume in the store downtown."

Dr. Harvey looked at his daughter. She was getting so grown up. "I thought you always made your costumes," he said.

"Mom did."

"Oh. Well let me see if I can put something together for you. Maybe we can roll you in aluminum foil," said her dad hopefully. "You could go as a leftover."

Kat gave him a sour look.

"Honey, don't worry. You always look cute." Dr. Harvey wondered what he had said wrong.

"I don't want to look *cute*—cute's like when you're nine years old with papier mâché around your head." Kat looked down, then right into her father's eyes. "I want to look nice. Like . . . date nice."

"Really?" Dr. Harvey was surprised. Was she that grown up already?

Kat nodded.

"Honey," Dr. Harvey said, coming over to Kat and holding her, "you know I'd like to buy you anything you want, but until Carrigan pays me, that card's pretty worthless."

Kat tried to hide her disappointment. "No biggee, Dad. I'm sure I'll come up with something for the party."

From somewhere in Whipstaff the sound of ghostly singing wailed through the air. "It's my party, and I'll die if I want to. Die if I want to. Die if I want to . . ." Stretch, Fatso, and Stinkie were up.

Kat groaned. "Dad, please, whatever you do, don't let those guys crash this Halloween party."

"Honey, I don't know if I can stop them," Dr. Harvey said, not looking at Kat. He was starting to feel a little hopeless about getting rid of the three semi-invisible pests. Out of the corner of his eye he saw the pitcher of orange juice. Suddenly he had an idea. He squared his shoulders with resolve. "I'll handle them. I promise."

Kat gave her dad a kiss and bounded back up the stairs. When Dr. Harvey turned around to finish pouring his coffee, it was just in time to see the brown liquid floating out of the pot and off into the other room.

———

Up at the very top floor of Whipstaff Manor was a grand old attic. Sunlight poured through dusty old slats in the windows, illuminating a maze of ancient boxes and crates, antique tables, and art deco furniture decades old.

Kat spotted a sliver of light coming from a crack in a nearby door. She pushed through a pile of junk and opened the door. What she saw made her gasp.

It was a large, circular room with tall windows all around. Though the windows here, too, were covered with dust, enough light came in to make the air glow with sparkling magic. A few feet from the ceiling was a shelf that circled the entire room. A dusty train sat on the track, looking as if it was waiting for a child that had never returned to play with it. Kat couldn't believe it—a hidden toy room!

She grabbed a sheet and pulled it off an interesting looking pile of boxes. She was straining to see what was inside so she walked over to the window to rub a clean spot for the sun to shine through. She crossed back across the room and cracked open the first box. The contents of the box made her smile. Wow!

Downstairs, the Ghostly Trio was having their own brand of fun. Each ghost was floating, holding a pen and a pad, pretending to be therapists themselves, when Dr. Harvey walked in.

"Vell, vell, ze patient has arrived. . . ." said Stretch.

"Late again," added Stinkie.

"Could this be an expression of hostility?" asked Stretch with a sneer.

"It's your hour," mocked Fatso. The three ghosts howled with laughter. But Dr. Harvey didn't react. He calmly crossed the room to his desk.

"What? So silent?" Stretch asked, confused. "No pearls of wisdom today, Doc?"

"C'mon, Doc. Stay tough, don't stuff," Stinkie advised. More laughter echoed through the room.

But Dr. Harvey ignored them. He began collecting his belongings and boxing them. The Trio frowned. What was their ghost shrink up to?

"Hey, wait a second, Doc," said Stretch. "You ain't thinkin' of packin' it in now, are ya?"

"We was just startin' to have fun," complained Fatso.

"It ain't often we meet a bonebag as amusin' as you," agreed Stinkie.

Dr. Harvey continued to pretend the ghosts were invisible as he kept packing. They were in a huddle, so they didn't catch his sneaky glances at them as he watched for their reactions. Dr. Harvey was using reverse psychology on them, trying to get them to want to be with him by ignoring them. But they didn't know that.

"Boys, this looks serious. I think Doc's havin' one of them fleshie breakdowns," Stretch said.

"Time for drastic measures," agreed Stinkie. It was decided. The Doc was in serious need of a ghostly prescription. The Trio swooped in and put their arms around Dr. Harvey.

As Dr. Harvey and the three ghosts swooped out the window, Carrigan and Dibs ducked. The Trio could be heard cackling in the distance.

"This is an outrage!" said Dibs, furious. "It's appalling. You pay a man to get the ghosts out of the house and what does he do—?"

"He gets the ghosts out of the house," replied Carrigan, smirking at her not-so-bright lawyer.

"Exactly," said Dibs. He began to hum as he formed a stirrup with his palms to boost Carrigan through the library window.

"God, you irritate me," complained Carrigan as she dug her high heel into Dibs' palm and pulled herself into the room.

11

The Ghostly Trio was not exactly known for its good house-keeping habits. And just that morning they had decided that Whipstaff's main room was too clean for their tastes. They had ordered Casper to mess it up. Messing up consisted of using a feather duster to spread dust all over the place. But before Casper could get started, he heard, somewhere in the manor, the sound of a toy calliope twinkling merrily. Casper floated off to investigate.

Through the walls and floors into the attic he flew. The music was coming from the old toy room! Casper slipped through the crack in the door.

The toy room windows were now sparkling clean. And what was even better, hundreds of moving antique toys were wound into action, filling the room with music and motion.

Kat smiled up at Casper's astonished face.

The friendly ghost floated over the toys. Joy and wonder filled his face, as he floated toward a plaster hand print hung on the wall. He placed his hand up to the plaster hand print. "This is . . ." he began. Suddenly he froze. "I remember!"

Casper flew in a circle around the room, laughing playfully, looking at everything. He stopped in front of a bookshelf. "I remember I used to stay up way past my bed-time and sneak read *Treasure Island*. . . ." The toot of a train interrupted him. He flew over to the train on the shelf track above Kat. "Hoonie!"

Then Casper dove into a trunk—through the lid, of course. After a minute, it opened and Casper emerged. Kat could not take her eyes off of what he held in his hand. It was an ancient, antique lace dress!

"Hands up, Kat," said Casper. She raised her hands and he let the dress float down over her head.

Kat touched the dress and looked up at Casper. "It's fantastic!"

"It was my mom's," said Casper.

Kat moved toward the mirror and pulled the waist of the dress in. "It's so perfect!" she cried. "Casper, do you mind if I wear it to the party?" Casper didn't answer. Kat turned around to see him seated on a small red sled. Casper looked so small and sad.

"I begged and begged my dad to get me a sled and he acted like I couldn't have one 'cuz I didn't know how to ride it. And one morning I came down for breakfast and there it was for me. For no reason at all." Casper was remembering his life for the first time since he had died. "I took it out and went sledding all day. My dad said I had been out enough. But I couldn't stop playing. I was having so much fun. And it got late, and it got dark, and it got cold, and I got sick. And my dad—got sad."

"What's it like to die, Casper?" asked Kat her eyes wide.

Casper thought for a moment. "Like being born, only backward. I remember I didn't go where I was supposed to when I died. I stayed behind so my dad wouldn't be lonely."

As Kat listened, she sifted through some dusty, yellowed newspapers on the floor. She lifted up an ancient article. The headline read: "PROMINENT INVENTOR, J. T. MCFADDEN DECLARED LEGALLY INSANE."

Kat read aloud: "McFadden claimed that he was haunted by the ghost of his dead son and that he had invented a machine to bring him back to life: The Lazarus."

"The Lazarus!" exclaimed Casper. He grabbed her hand and flew right through the toy room wall. Kat hit the wall and fell to the floor in a heap. "Sorry," said Casper, floating back into the room to retrieve Kat. "We'll take the long way."

Casper and Kat raced down the spiral staircase and into the hall. "My dad hid the Lazarus so no one could find it," said Casper. "But I remember where it is! Wait till you see it!"

Hiding in the shadows, Carrigan and Dibs heard what Casper said about the Lazarus. Carrigan was so excited about finding the missing treasure that she kissed Dibs on the lips. Dibs closed his eyes and stood there, still kissing her back, but Carrigan had already left the room, following the sound of Casper's voice. Dibs fell over, lips first. He quickly picked himself up and raced after her.

Casper zoomed into the library with Kat in tow. Just as he was about to float through the wall, it opened up to reveal a hidden balcony on the second floor of the library. "Sit down," Casper said, pointing to an overstuffed armchair.

Kat sat. Casper flew over to a lamp and pulled one of the crystals hanging from it. The chair lurched into motion—backward! Kat hung on tightly as the chair quickly moved along a track embedded in the floor. At the end of the balcony was a spiral staircase that went down to the lower level of the library.

Kat was getting nervous as the chair got closer to the stairs. "Hang on!" yelled Casper. Suddenly the chair turned around. The stairs on the spiral staircase flattened against each other and became a ramp. Kat screamed as the chair flew downward. Just as the chair was about to crash at the bottom of the spiral, a circular door opened.

Carrigan and Dibs were watching the entire scene. They raced after Dr. Harvey's daughter and her friend, the little ghost. There was no way Carrigan was going to let a bratty little girl steal the treasure that belonged to her!

12

The chair lurched down, down, down, along the track. An assembly line of robot arms reached out to her. Kat reached up to touch the robots. Gloved metallic hands applied shaving cream to her face. She ducked just before the razor shaved her face. A towel wiped off the excess shaving cream. More arms applied grease to her hair, while a gloved hand with a comb slicked her hair back. Robot hands brushed her teeth and polished her sneakers, then attached a bow tie to her. The chair continued down into an underground laboratory.

The tracks passed over a canal of sea water and the chair stopped at the island of inventions at the center of the room. Kat got up and looked around. The fantastic room was built into the cliff under Whipstaff Manor. Beakers lined the walls. Papers of invention plans lay scattered about. A chalkboard was filled with magical formulas and in the middle of the room was a pool.

Casper looked at Kat with her lace dress, polished sneakers, bow tie, and slicked down hair parted down the middle. He laughed.

"What was that?" she asked, referring to the machine with all the arms.

"The Up and At 'Em Machine. My dad was a great inventor, but he had a little trouble getting up in the morning," explained Casper.

"Didn't he ever hear of cappuccino?" Kat asked.

Suddenly the chair began to back up. Someone was on their trail. They had to move fast before they were discovered.

In the library, Carrigan had just tugged on the crystal in the lamp that triggered the chair. Dibs was suddenly scooped up onto Carrigan's lap as the chair appeared and flew backward. The two of them went shooting down the spiral staircase and through the floor!

Carrigan didn't like the Up and At 'Em Machine. She kicked at the robot arms and caused the machine to malfunction. A toothbrush full of toothpaste brushed her ears. Hands rubbed hair grease on her shirt and the comb raked over it. Shaving lather was shoved straight into her mouth.

The razor went straight for Dibs' face. Would he duck in time?

"So where is this Lazarus thing?" Kat asked Casper, looking around the lab.

"You're looking at it," said Casper.

Kat stared at the pool. She could see something in the water. How were they going to get at it? Kat pointed to a large, rusted door embedded in the cave wall. "What about that?"

"That's the vault," said Casper.

Kat crossed to the desk searching for clues. Sifting through items on the desk, she came across an old book and blew dust off the cover. It was Mary Shelley's *Frankenstein!* She opened the cover and found three buttons hidden inside. One was taller than the other two. She pressed it and the sound of hydraulic power suddenly filled the room.

"Hey! I did it!" yelled Casper from across the room. Kat smiled to herself—why burst his bubble?

The pool in the center of the room began to bubble. A geyser erupted, sending steaming water shooting into the air. Something began to rise from the steam of the geyser. Kat and

Casper jumped back as a spherical chamber arose from the pool. Wires, tubes, and pipes surrounded it, and steel steps appeared along a track leading from the shore up to the chamber. With a loud sucking sound, a vacuum seal on the chamber door opened.

"The Lazarus!" stated Casper.

Dibs and Carrigan were skulking along the wall, hidden in the shadows. Once they heard the word vault, they had been waiting for the perfect time to jump in on Kat and Casper. But they had never expected to see that contraption rising from the water.

"And this was supposed to bring you back to life?" asked Kat.

"My dad got sent away before he could use it on me," Casper said.

Kat walked toward what looked like the main controls. In a small, box-like holder was a single red vial. Most of the gel inside the vial looked like it had leaked out. Kat picked it up and shook it. "What's this?" she asked.

Casper swooped in and plucked the red vial from her hand. "Careful! That's what makes it work." Kat didn't get it. "It's what brings ghosts back to life. Just enough for one."

Casper looked at the vial thoughtfully then made a decision. He flew the vial over to a slot on the Lazarus and stuck it in. Kat watched, realizing the importance of what he was about to do. Casper opened the door to the Lazarus chamber, looking back at Kat.

"Pull the lever," he said. "I'm gonna be alive." He closed the chamber door.

Kat stepped up to the control panel. "How am I going to do this?" she said softly, feeling panicked. "I couldn't even get a toy baking oven to work." She found a lever and pulled it, hoping it was the right one. The Lazarus began to shake and roar. Steam rose from its top. Either it was working or it was self-destructing, she didn't know which one.

All of a sudden, Carrigan, who had been hiding in the shadows, reached into the slot for the red vial and yanked it out! The Lazarus coughed, sputtered, and stalled. Kat rushed over to Casper and gasped, horrified. She was staring at a jelly-like blob with eyes.

"Am I alive?" marveled Casper.

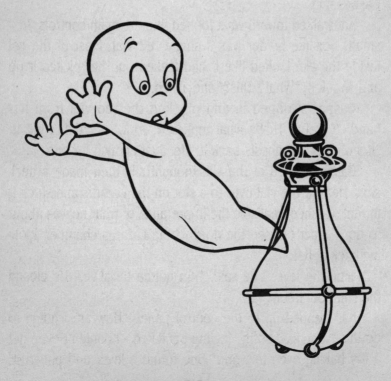

13

In a restaurant not far from Whipstaff, Dr. Harvey and the Ghostly Trio were having a blast. The restaurant, though, looked like a cattle stampede had galloped through it. Tables were overturned, chairs lay upside-down, food was splattered about. But the good doctor and the three uncles didn't notice a thing.

Dr. Harvey had just finished singing a song. The Ghostly Trio applauded his performance, and he took a bow. "Thank you, thank you. You kids are the greatest audience I ever had. . . . Any song requests?"

Stretch spoke. "I say we get outta here."

Dr. Harvey turned to them in protest. "No way! Remember? We're making this a night to remember!" He strode over to the jukebox and slipped in a coin. A slow, heartbreaking ballad came on.

Dr. Harvey was overcome with emotion. "Can I just say something here? Get a little personal? The past few years I've gone through a lot. We've been moving around a whole bunch and I know it's been hard on Kat. She hasn't been able to make any friends . . ." Dr. Harvey started to tear up. "But you know what? Tonight I realized that neither have I! Without Kat, I'm alone in this world. The reason I haven't been able to hang out with my buddies is because I don't *have* any!" Dr. Harvey went over to the Trio and put his arms around them, "Until now. Seriously," he sniffled, "you guys remind me of what good times really are. . . ."

The Ghostly Trio began to cry.

Dr. Harvey continued, ". . . I'm going to tell that Miss Carrigan that you don't want to move on. It's your house. You're haunting it and you have every legal right to! You guys are the best! I love you guys!"

The Trio was sobbing for real. What was this world coming to? And what on earth was the matter with Dr. Harvey? Before they had time to think, Dr. Harvey marched out of the restaurant—right toward a construction sign that read: OPEN TRENCH. Seconds later, they heard a horrible wail and a loud thud. The three ghosts looked at one another and at the trench. Was that a ghost they saw coming out of the hole or what?

When Dibs saw Carrigan snatch the vial out of the lumbering Lazarus, he ran to follow her. Neither of them paid any attention to the blob that Casper now was. Once they reached the mansion hallway, they stopped, and Carrigan finally spoke.

"Dibs, do you have any idea what this means?" she said excitedly, shaking the vial at him.

"Yes! No?" he answered

"No more fear of death!" said Carrigan. "One minute you're a ghost, the next you're back on your feet—free to come and go as you please!"

"Heck," Dibs agreed, "you could even fly through . . ."

" . . . walls," she finished for him. "And whatever treasure lay behind those walls would be yours. I mean mine. Uh, ours. If you were a ghost, that is."

"If *you* were," Dibs said.

"No, if *you* were," she replied, and promptly pushed Dibs off the balcony! Dibs flipped mid-air and landed on the banister, plopping painfully down the railing until he crashed into a stone fish head at the end of the railing. If pain could cause humans to see stars, Dibs was sure he was seeing entire galaxies.

Carrigan stood at the top of the stairs, laughing hysterically, and watching Dibs slowly remove himself from the banister. Before she could take another breath, Dibs pulled out the carpet from under her feet. Carrigan came tumbling off the balcony and landed in a couch. Dibs ran for his life. Carrigan raced after him.

Into the library they ran. "Come out, come out wherever you are," called out Carrigan. Where was that Dibs?

Dibs raced out to the driveway, where he spotted the red vial. He moved to grab it when all of a sudden, headlights lit him up. Carrigan gunned the engine as her car sprang to life—right toward Dibs.

"Nooooo!" screamed Dibs.

Inside the car, Carrigan muttered to herself, "Dibs, you're taking this way too personally." Before she could stop, the car hit a tree. The airbag inflated, saving her life. She stepped out of the car. Unfortunately, she didn't see that the smashed car was perched over the cliff. Out she stepped—and down she fell to the churning waters below.

Dibs ran over to the edge of the cliff. "Carrigan?" he called down after her. "Are you a ghost yet? Carrigan?" No answer. He stepped away from the cliff.

"Not so fast, little man!" came a monstrous voice.

Dibs gaped and looked up. There was Carrigan, a huge, fearsome ghost floating in the air above him.

"I'm back!" she warned menacingly.

Still in the hidden lab, Kat tried to fix Casper the blob. She tried to blow him back into shape with an old fireplace bellows. But all she did was make his ears pop.

As she stood there, trying to figure out how to cure Casper of his blobbiness, a huge ghostly form rushed over their heads and disappeared through the vault door in the wall, without opening it! The sound of crazy laughter crept out under the vault door. The handle of the vault door turned and out floated Carrigan, holding an old treasure chest that looked like it belonged to a pirate.

"My treasure!" yelled Casper.

"You mean *my* treasure," answered Carrigan.

Just then Dibs came running down into the room holding the precious red vial in his hand.

"Hey! You stole that!" Kat cried. "That's Casper's!"

"So sue me," said Carrigan nastily. She dropped the treasure chest down next to the Lazarus and flung open the Lazarus chamber door. The traveling chair docked at the edge, ready for a passenger.

Casper floated behind Dibs and yanked him by the tie. Dibs flailed. Kat saw her chance. She grabbed the vial from his hand. Then Casper pushed Dibs into the canal.

"Jump in!" yelled Casper to Kat.

Kat sat in the chair and Casper pushed it quickly up the track. Faster than a flying bullet they sped through the tunnel, up and around the spiral staircase, and across the balcony into the library. Just then the doorbell rang.

"Oh, perfect," said Kat in dismay. She had totally forgotten. Her entire class had just arrived at Whipstaff for the Halloween dance.

14

Kat opened the door to a flock of costumed students loaded down with party supplies. They all stood there waiting for her to invite them in. Mr. Curtis was dressed in a homemade lobster outfit.

"So, where's the butter? Get it? Lobster? Butter?" Mr. Curtis laughed.

Kat spoke fast. "Come on in. This is the room. Stay together. I'll be right back." And she raced upstairs.

Downstairs, the kids were all looking upstairs toward the hidden commotion. Crashes and shrieks echoed through the house.

"Wow," said one student, "serious sound effects."

Kat ran into the library and closed the door behind her. As Casper and Kat disappeared into the lab tunnel, two shadowy figures crept in through the open library window. Dressed up as ghosts and covered with fake blood, Amber and Vic landed on the floor.

"Amber, isn't it enough that we're standing her up in front of the whole school?" said Vic.

"*We're* not," replied Amber, "*you* are. Come on, let's get ready." Amber was looking forward to revenge.

Heaving against a crowbar, Dibs tried desperately to pry open the lid of the treasure chest. Kat and Casper slid into the lab, startling Dibs. He waved the crowbar at them.

"Stay back! Don't come near me!" he warned.

"That's my treasure!" yelled Casper.

"Forget about it, Casper," said Kat. "Come on!" Kat loaded the vial into the Lazarus. She looked at Casper. This was it. Casper would finally be alive! Casper opened the door of the Lazarus and out floated Carrigan!

"Dibs!" Carrigan ordered. "Get this thing cookin'!"

But Dibs had other ideas. Calmly, he walked over to the Lazarus' control panel and removed the red vial. "Carrigan," he said, "if there's one thing I've learned from you, it's kick 'em when they're down, and baby, you're six feet under— we're through!"

"I'm not going to forget this, you ungrateful . . ." Carrigan hissed.

"You can haunt me all you want, but it's gonna be in a big, expensive house. I got the power. I got the treasure!" Dibs gloated.

Carrigan inhaled and blew Dibs straight up and out through a skylight. He was never heard from again.

Carrigan had blown with such force that the vial hung suspended in the air long enough for her to grab it. She whirled on Casper and Kat. "Any other takers?"

"No," said Casper. "But aren't you forgetting your unfinished business?"

"My what?"

"All ghosts have unfinished business," Kat said.

"That's why we're ghosts," Casper agreed.

Carrigan floated over to the treasure chest, grabbing it up. "I've got my treasure. I've got everything. I have no unfinished business!"

Suddenly Carrigan began to smoke and shake. She dropped the treasure chest, clutched her throat and started to rapidly shrink! With more smoke, a roar, and a poof! Carrigan was gone. Forever.

Kat dove and caught the vial before it hit the ground.

"My treasure!" said Casper and reached into the treasure chest which had opened on impact. He pulled out an old, scuffed baseball.

"*That's* your treasure?" Kat said, amazed.

"Are you kidding?" Casper said. "It's autographed by Dan Brouthers of the Brooklyn Dodgers. My favorite player."

Kat looked warmly at Casper. This was fun but they had some de-ghosting to do. "Casper, it's time."

Casper nodded and made his way over to the Lazarus chamber while Kat reinserted the vial. Just as Kat was about to pull the lever, she heard, "Honey, I'm home!"

She and Casper spun around. At the edge of the canal stood Dr. Harvey. He was a ghost! The Ghostly Trio popped in behind him.

"Dad!" Kat screamed. "No! What did you do to him?"

"Nothin'!" said Stretch. "He's just a little dead. . . ."

"I'm free," said Dr. Harvey with a brilliant smile. "I've never felt so alive! And I can fly!" Dr. Harvey jumped in the air, about to do a ghost acrobatic trick, when he suddenly stopped and squinted at Kat. "Who's the girl?"

Kat's voice trembled. "DAAAAD! It's me! Kat!"

"Kat? Kat? Ah yes, Kat! Katacomb! Katalina Island! Katamaran!" chanted the ghostly Dr. Harvey. The three uncles begin to chant and tease Kat.

She was destroyed. How could her dad not know who she was? She held up her pinkie in their secret "OK" sign. "Dad, don't you remember?"

Dr. Harvey started to crack a joke, but suddenly, something dawned on his ghostly brain. Then his face registered it. He knew who she was. "Sweetheart . . . what have I done? Don't cry, Kat, please," begged Dr. Harvey.

Casper looked at Kat, then at Dr. Harvey, then at the Lazarus. He stared at the Lazarus. It really was a difficult decision to make.

Kat kept crying. Casper went over to Dr. Harvey, took him by the elbow and led him to the Lazarus chamber door. "Come on, Dr. Harvey. The living need you more than the dead. Let's get you back on your feet again." Casper floated Dr. Harvey into the chamber. He closed the door and joined Kat at the control panel.

"Casper . . ." began Kat.

"This is the way it's got to be," said Casper, and pulled the lever. The Lazarus rumbled, thundered, rocked, and steamed.

15

The Halloween party downstairs at Whipstaff Manor was growing by the minute. More and more kids streamed in through the door. Boys huddled in one corner and girls in another. It was a typical seventh-grade party—until the lights dimmed and the music started to warble. Something weird was definitely going on.

In the library, Amber stepped off a table onto Vic's shoulders. The lights then flickered off completely throughout the house. In the darkness, a scream echoed throughout the house.

A few tense minutes passed. The lights came back on. The chamber doors of the Lazarus machine flew open and Dr. Harvey stepped out, alive and real!

"Dad!" said Kat.

"Kat?"

Kat rushed to him and hugged him for all she was worth. "Are you OK?" she asked.

"OK?" he said, smiling. "Sweetheart, I've never felt better!"

A loud rock and roll beat began to shake the house. Casper looked at Kat. "Your party's starting without you. Your date's probably waiting."

Kat reluctantly took her dad's hand. "Come on, honey, let's go," Dr. Harvey said. He walked her over to the top of the stairs. "You go on," he urged Kat.

"What about you?" asked Kat.

"This is your party. Go do your thing. Go hang, or chill, or kick it, or whatever it is. Go find your date!" Dr. Harvey said.

Kat hesitated, looking down at the sea of costumed heads.

She scanned the room for Vic. He was nowhere to be seen. Where was her date?

———

In the library, Amber was finally able to stand up on Vic's shoulders. "Hold still!" she hissed, wobbling.

"I'm trying. Could you possibly weigh a little more?" said Vic sarcastically.

"Shut up and get your head down!" Amber ordered.

"Can we do this already?" asked Vic. "You're gonna break my back." They had one long sheet hung over the two of them, making a tall, scary looking ghost-monster.

"I have to see how we look," said Amber, directing him toward the mirror. "Oh my! People are going to freak!"

"Let me see," said Vic, lifting up the bottom part of the sheet. "Cool!"

All of a sudden, a third face peered back at them from the mirror. It was Stretch. "Thank you," said Stretch with a ghostly sneer. Stinkie and Fatso joined in and turned Vic and Amber's reflections into theirs. The Ghostly Trio howled with laughter.

The Amber-Vic monster screamed at the top of its lungs and ran spastically across the room. The sea of kids parted as the monster headed for the party room. Amber slammed her head against the top of the door frame and got dragged out after Vic. The kids laughed and began applauding.

"Great party!"

———

The toy room had been a much merrier place earlier that day. Now Casper sat alone watching the train chug slowly around the track. Over and over again, Casper tossed his favorite treasure baseball up in the air and caught it in his mitt. Up went the ball, and . . . it didn't come down.

Casper looked up. There floated Amelia, Kat's mom.

Unlike the photograph on Kat's bedside table, Amelia glowed with an angelic, otherworldly light.

"You're . . ." said Casper.

"Yes," said Amelia.

"Are you an angel?" asked Casper.

Amelia smiled sweetly in response. "That was a very noble thing you did tonight, Casper. I know Kat will never forget it." Casper looked down humbly. "And for what you've done, I'm giving you your dream in return."

Casper's face lit up.

"But it's just for tonight. Sort of a Cinderella deal," said Amelia.

"So I have until midnight?" asked Casper.

"Ten," said Amelia.

"But Cinderella got till midnight," protested Casper.

"Cinderella wasn't twelve years old," said Amelia. She passed an angelically lit hand slowly over Casper.

Downstairs, a fast song ended and the kids applauded each other. A slow song began and couples formed on the floor. Kat sat alone in a chair in the corner. She looked very sad.

At the top of the stairs, a handsome boy in a pirate costume bounded down the stairs. All the girls watched him. He was really cute! He walked straight over to Kat and smiled. Without saying a word, he extended his hand. He wanted to dance with her!

Kat was thrilled. She didn't say a word either, just took his hand and walked out onto the dance floor. They swayed to the music. He smiled at her again. Kat smiled back. But something looked strangely familiar about him.

"Told you I was a good dancer," Casper said.

Kat's eyes got big as she realized who this dashing pirate really was.

"And I'm gonna keep you!" said Casper.

"Casper?" said Kat in disbelief.

Casper smiled and pulled her closer to him. They rested their heads on each other's shoulders and danced and danced.

From where he stood above on the stairwell, Dr. Harvey looked down at his little girl. He didn't see the angelic figure drifting over next to him.

"She's growing up pretty," said Amelia.

"She sure . . ." Dr. Harvey turned, and then he saw her— his wife!

Amelia smiled. "Hello, James."

"Amelia?" Dr. Harvey was so shocked he could barely speak. "How? . . ."

"Let's just say you know three crazy ghosts who kept their word."

Dr. Harvey was overwhelmed. His wife! Finally! "Look how beautiful you are," he marveled.

"James, I know you've been searching for me. And I know you believe it's all been for Kat's sake," she said. "But you and I both know it's really been about you." Dr. Harvey was silent, listening. "James, you've got to understand something. You and Kat loved me so well when I was alive that I have no unfinished business. Please don't make me yours."

Dr. Harvey stared into her eyes. "But Amelia," protested Dr. Harvey, "I don't know what I'm doing."

"What parent does?" she answered.

"But Kat needs . . ."

"She needs her father," said Amelia warmly. "James, every decision you'll ever need to make is right inside of you. Kat's growing up beautifully because of you."

Dr. Harvey eyed her achingly.

"Just a couple of things, though," she added. "Don't pick up the extension every time she gets a phone call. French fries aren't a breakfast food. And don't ask her to wear a T-shirt under her bathing suit—I mean, c'mon, James, the girl is a teenager." Amelia smiled.

Dr. Harvey looked into his wife's eyes. He reached up to stroke her glowing face. "No wonder I miss you so much." Suddenly the grandfather clock began to strike ten. Amelia began to fade away.

"Wait!" protested Dr. Harvey. "Where are you going?"

"Where I can watch over both of you . . . until we're together again." Dr. Harvey's eyes began filling with tears. "Good-bye, James." Her glow grew even more brilliant, then burst into a soft shower of light. She was gone. Dr. Harvey looked downstairs at the dance floor through his tears.

When the clock began to strike, Casper lifted his head off of Kat's shoulder and smiled. He knew it was time. He looked into Kat's tilted face until she met his eyes.

"Casper? . . ." she began. As the last stroke of the clock sounded, Casper slowly leaned in and gently kissed Kat. Within seconds he had faded back into a ghost.

When Kat opened her eyes again, she saw nearly every kid in the room with an open mouth, staring at Casper. They could not believe what they thought they were seeing. Casper smiled his friendly little ghost smile, shrugged, and said, "Boo?"

All at once everyone on the floor erupted into the biggest scream imaginable. They ran, hollering and yelling, stampeding for the door. Kat and Casper were soon alone on the dance floor.

"Not bad for our first party, huh?" said Kat.

Casper smiled. "They'll never forget it in this town."

"It ain't over yet," called out Dr. Harvey from the bottom of the stairs. "Hit it, boys!"

Over in the other side of the room, nearly hidden by a pile of drums and guitars, the Ghostly Trio waited. They launched into a jammin' dance number. Dr. Harvey and Kat began to dance.

Casper, filled with joy, soared through the air up above them. Kat watched him happily as he floated away. Before he disappeared, he gave her one big, friendly, ghost-wink.

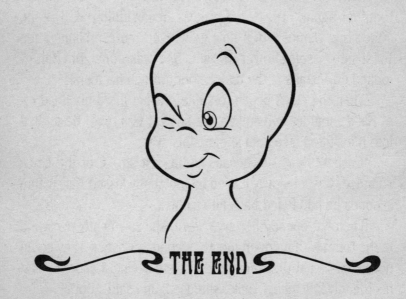

THE END